P9-CTQ-164

PALM BEACH COUNTY
LIBRARY SYSTEM
3650 Summit Boulevard
West Palm Beach, FL 33406-4198

For my wonderful mum who, when she woke up, was not a hippopotamus. T.M.

For Sabine, Lonneke, Jessie, and Max. R.C.

American edition published in 2011 by Andersen Press USA, an imprint of Andersen Press Ltd.
www.andersenpressusa.com

First published in Great Britain in 2011 by Andersen Press Ltd.,
20 Vauxhall Bridge Road, London SW1V 2SA.
Published in Australia by Random House Australia Pty.,
Level 3, 100 Pacific Highway, North Sydney, NSW 2060.

Text copyright © Tom MacRae, 2011.
Illustration copyright © Ross Collins, 2011.

The rights of Tom MacRae and Ross Collins to be identified as the author and illustrator of this work have been asserted by them
in accordance with the Copyright, Designs and Patents Act, 1988. All rights reserved. No part of this book may be reproduced, stored
in a retrieval system, or transmitted in any form or by any means—electronic, mechanical, photocopying, recording, or otherwise—without
the prior written permission of Andersen Press Ltd., except for the inclusion of brief quotations in an acknowledged review.

Distributed in the United States and Canada by
Lerner Publishing Group, Inc.
241 First Avenue North
Minneapolis, MN 55401 U.S.A.
www.lernerbooks.com

Library of Congress Cataloging-in-Publication Data Available.
ISBN: 978-0-7613-8099-3

Color separated in Switzerland by Photolitho AG, Zürich. Printed and bound in Singapore by Tien Wah Press.
Ross Collins has used concentrated watercolor, vinyl color, and pen on watercolor paper in this book.

1 - TWP - 3/7/11

WHEN I WOKE UP I WAS A HIPPOPOTAMUS

Tom MacRae

Ross Collins

ANDERSEN PRESS USA

When I woke up, I was a

hippopotamus.

Yawning in the morning, I raised up my sleepy head,
then took one look out of the window
and got straight back into bed.

"Get up!" said Mom. "Or you'll be late!"

But hippos in their sludge
don't get up in the morning,
and so I didn't budge.

My tummy wasn't hungry. I wasn't programmed how to eat.
My mouth was made of metal, like my nose and knees and feet.
"Quick, quick!" said Dad. "Come on! Eat up!
We've really got to scoot!"

But robots can't eat
cornflakes. Dad's words
did not compute.

When it was time to go to school, I was a . . .

STATUE.

I couldn't move a muscle.
I couldn't blink an eye.
I couldn't lift a finger.
I couldn't breathe a sigh.

Mom pushed, then pulled.
Dad pulled, then pushed.
They heaved with all their might.

But my legs were made of granite
and my feet were stuck down tight.

When I got to school, I was a . . .
Monkey!

A cheeky little monkey
thought a table was a tree.
I had to climb upon it just to
see what I could see.

I couldn't sit and listen,
and my work was rather slack.
And when the teacher told me off—
I told her off right back!

When it was playtime, I was a . . .

MONSTER!

A scritchy-scratchy monster with ten scritchy-scratchy claws.
I had fifty scritchy-scratchy teeth in scritchy-scratchy jaws.

The girls all screamed! The boys all ran!
My mouth went munchy-crunch!
Then teacher told me off again
(so I had her for my lunch).

I zoomed up out of orbit,
countdown—5, 4, 3, 2, 1.
I was nearly reaching light speed.
Poor old Dad, he had to run!

My pistons pumped,
my jet packs jumped—
all full of super fuel.
I had to get to Planet Home
and far from Planet School!

When I was in my bedroom I was a . . . GIANT!
My hands were huge as houses, my beard was big and blue.
I was hunting for a human to put in my human stew.
I was crashing 'round my bedroom —well that's just how giants play.
We're big and loud and noisy. We don't know another way.

But Mom and Dad weren't happy, and they yelled out, "Keep it down!"

But my giant feet were busy as they crushed a tiny town.
"That's it!" cried Mom and Dad.
"You're louder than TEN boys!"
And they stomped upstairs to tell me off
for making so much noise.

When Mom and Dad came in, they were ...DRAGONS!

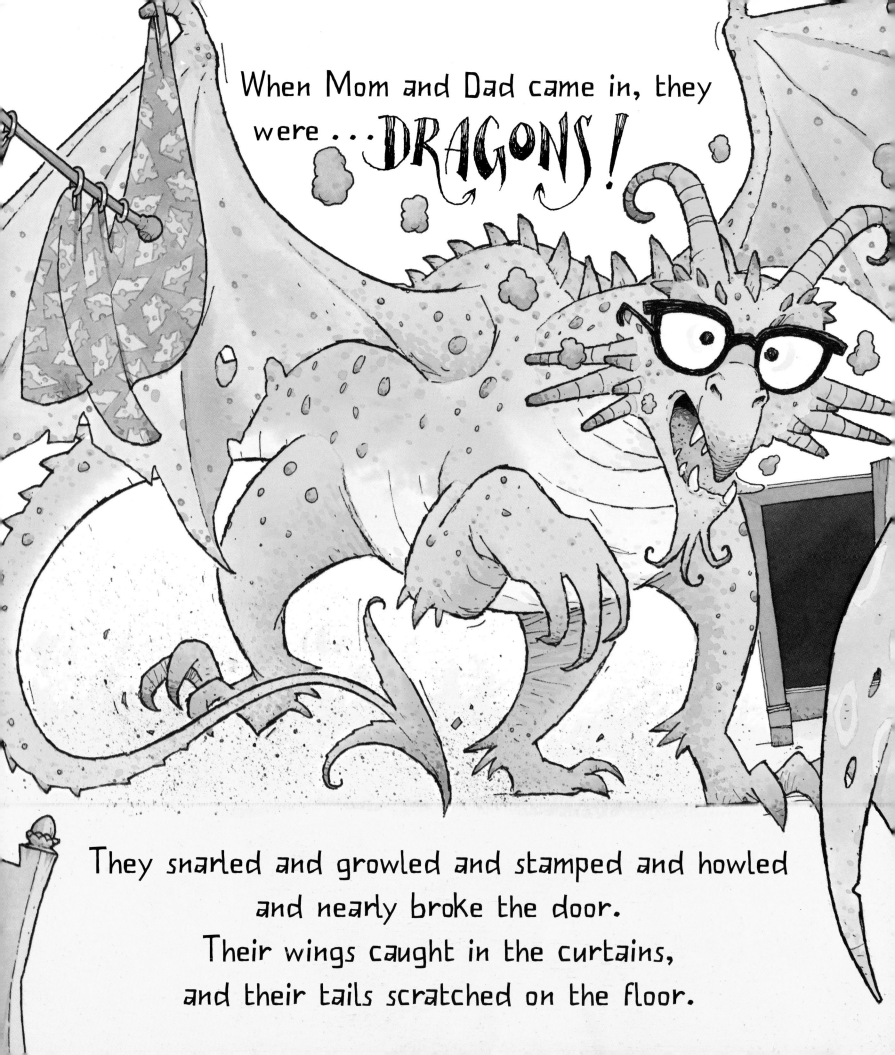

They snarled and growled and stamped and howled
and nearly broke the door.
Their wings caught in the curtains,
and their tails scratched on the floor.

Dad blew a giant smoke ring
with an angry rumbling cough.
Mom wagged a scaly finger—
    then they *really* told me off!

I stared up at my mom and dad
and didn't feel so brave.

I was having fun pretending—
I didn't mean to misbehave.

"Of all the wondrous things," said
Mom, "that you pretend to be,

why can't you be a *nice* thing?"

So I pretended I was . . .

...ME!

We had a lovely evening.
I helped my dad with tea.

Then I read my mom
a story as I sat
upon her knee.

At bath time we played pirates and we plotted pirate schemes.

Then I snuggled in my blanket . . .

...and dreamed AMAZING DREAMS.